The
Witch Dog

The Witch Dog

Written by
Margaret Mahy

Illustrated by
Sam Usher

Orion
Children's Books

The Witch Dog originally appeared in
The First Margaret Mahy Storybook
first published in Great Britain in 1972
by J.M. Dent & Sons
This abridged Early Reader edition
first published in Great Britain in 2014
by Orion Children's Books
a division of the Orion Publishing Group Ltd
Orion House
5 Upper Saint Martin's Lane
London WC2H 9EA
An Hachette UK Company

1 3 5 7 9 10 8 6 4 2

A catalogue record for this book is available from the British Library.

ISBN 978 1 4440 1134 0

Printed and bound in China

www.orionbooks.co.uk

There was once a mum whose children had all grown up.

This mum now had nothing to do but tidy her tidy house and weed her neat garden. This was not very interesting for her.

So, one day, this mum – her name was Mrs Rose – said to her husband, "I think I'll join a club or take a class."

"That's a good idea," said Mr Rose. "How about playing bowls?" (He played bowls himself, you see.)

"No, I don't fancy that," said Mrs Rose.

"I think I'll learn to be a witch. I saw in the paper that they are having classes at night school."

Mrs Rose turned out to be a very good witch. She found it easy.

The Head Witch was pleased. "Witch Rose," she said, "you are doing **excellently**."

"You can come and dance at our Witch Dance as soon as you can fly a broomstick."

Mrs Rose was delighted – she was the only one in the class to be invited.

She worked hard with her
broomstick.

First she learned to balance
and then to soar, and soon she
was soaring and swooping in
the wind.

"Well, Witch Rose," said the Head Witch, "you're a star pupil. Next Friday you can come to our Witch Dance. You must make a cloak and hat and get a cat, too."

Mrs Rose looked worried.

"A cat!" she said, but the
Head Witch had rushed off.

"A cat!" muttered Mrs Rose,
for there was

 something

she hadn't told the Head Witch

 – something

she hadn't even thought about,

 something

that meant perhaps that she
could never ever be a true witch
and dance at the Witch Dances.

"What am I going to do?"
she cried to Mr Rose. "Cat's fur
makes me sneeze. I won't be
able to go. Even a kitten makes
me sneeze."

"Get a dog," said Mr Rose. "A small dog – that will fit on the end of a broomstick. Dogs don't make you sneeze."

"Oh," Mrs Rose said. "I wonder . . . That's a good idea. I'll think about it."

She didn't have to think long, for the first thing she saw when she went out next morning was a funny little lost dog.

He had no collar but looked
cheerful and Mrs Rose liked
him at once.

She liked his silvery grey coat, and she liked his ears which stuck up into the air and then hung down at the tips.

"Would you like to be a witch dog?" Mrs Rose asked him, and he wriggled his nose and wagged his tail.

"Very well," said Mrs Rose.
"I will call you Nightshade.
That's a good witch name."

On Friday night Mrs Rose
put on her hat and cloak
and tucked her wand into
her belt. She climbed onto
her broomstick. Nightshade
hopped on behind.

A moment later they were in the air and Mrs Rose pointed her broomstick towards Miller's Hill.

Already Miller's Hill was
bustling and rustling with
witches – lots of witches.

They were standing around
a huge fire, some with cats and
some with owls.

When Mrs Rose and
Nightshade glided down they
were quiet . . .

. . . except for the usual witch
noises like muttering, cackling
and screaming.

But then there was scratching and shouting, and the cats put out their claws, puffed up their fur and shot off to climb trees.

The owls took off in a whirl
of angry feathers.

The Head Witch came down.
"What are you up to, Witch
Rose? A witch can be wicked –
but **never, never** stupid!

Why are you bringing a dog
to our dance?"

"Well," said Mrs Rose, "the
fact is, cats make me sneeze.
They make me sneeze terribly."

"I'm sure Nightshade will make a splendid witch dog, Head Witch, and once the cats get used to him . . ."

The Head Witch was about
to interrupt, when a surprising
thing happened.

A large toad, as big as a cat, hopped into the circle of witches.

Their squeaking, squealing and cackling stopped and they stared long and hard at the toad.

Even Mrs Rose could see that it was no ordinary toad, but an enchanted witch.

"Goodness gracious, it's Witch Smudge!" cried the Head Witch. "I must see what's wrong. I'll deal with your problem later, Witch Rose."

She turned to the toad. "Smudge, what are you doing here looking like that? Is it a joke?"

The toad croaked.

"What?" said the Head Witch.
"Smudge, you are a fool!"
She turned to the other
witches. "Witch Smudge has
been enchanted for a month.

It must have been an old-fashioned sort of enchanter to turn her into a toad – but he made a good job of it and there's nothing we can do.

I only wish he'd turned her into a plate of sausages."

A great **groaning** and
moaning and **howling**
burst forth from the witches
and rose up to the moon.

"The fact is," the Head Witch said to Mrs Rose, "Witch Smudge is one of the liveliest, wickedest witches in our group. She plays the liveliest, wickedest witch music. It's a delight to dance to her tunes …

And now, she's been turned
into a toad, the selfish creature.
I don't see what we are going
to do."

But then, Mrs Rose's silvery dog, Nightshade, sat back on his hind legs and whipped out a little violin made of silvery wood with three green strings and one golden one.

He snatched a twig of golden rod, and played a few notes of the maddest, wickedest witch-music you ever heard.

The witches began to jig and kick, showing their red-and-black striped stockings.

Then Nightshade really
began to play, and the witches
whirled and swirled.

The owls spun and spiralled
in the night air,

and the cats crouched in the
shadows.

When at last it stopped, all the witches, owls and cats fell in a heap, legs kicking in all directions.

The Head Witch felt around among the cats and owls and the other witches until she found Mrs Rose. They shook hands warmly.

"That was no ordinary music," said the Head Witch. "And you are no ordinary witch, Witch Rose. You can keep your dog, and we'll give him the title of **Witch-Cat Extraordinary.**"

So that is why, whenever the witches meet on Miller's Hill, Mrs Rose is always dancing among them – one of the best witches to come out of night school.

And, playing the music on his fiddle, Nightshade dances too – the first dog ever to become a witch cat.

What are you going to read next?

Have more adventures with Horrid Henry,

or save the day with Anthony Ant!

Become a
superhero with Monstar,

float off to
sea with Algy,

or have your very own Pirates' Picnic.

Grow carrots with

Lottie and Dottie,

make magic with
The Witch Dog,

and cast a spell with
The Three
Little Magicians.

Enjoy all the Early Readers.